# JAMES STEVENSON

We Can't Sleep

Greenwillow Books, New York

Library of Congress
Cataloging in Publication Data

Stevenson, James (date)
We can't sleep.
Summary:
Grandpa's rather unusual cure
for his sleeplessness seems to
work on others as well.
[1. Sleep–Fiction.
2. Humorous stories]
I. Title.
PZ7.S84748We    [E]    81-20307
ISBN 0-688-01213-2    AACR2
ISBN 0-688-01214-0 (lib. bdg.)

"We can't sleep," said Louie.

"Oh?" said Grandpa. "What seems to be the trouble?"

"It's too hot and quiet," said Mary Ann.

"Too windy and noisy," said Louie.

"Too light."

"Too dark."

"Too lonely."

"We just can't *sleep*," said Mary Ann.

"That's strange," said Grandpa.
"I once had that very same problem.

It was many years ago.
I was about your age.

I tossed and turned. I counted sheep. Nothing helped.

Finally, I got up, got dressed, and went outside. Maybe exercise would help.

I ran fifty miles...all uphill!"

"Did that make you sleepy, Grandpa?" asked Mary Ann.

"No," said Grandpa, "but it made me hot.

I decided to go for a swim and cool off.

The water felt good, so I decided
to swim across the ocean.

Sometimes the waves were enormous..."

"Were there any sharks?"
asked Louie.
"A great many," said Grandpa.

"They swam right at me. But...

as they came by, I dove down,

grabbed the tail of one,

and when he flipped his tail, I went up in the air,

and grabbed his fin.

I had a good, fast ride, and
they never did see me.

When I saw an iceberg,
I let go of the shark.

I swam to the iceberg..."

"You must have been pretty
tired," said Louie.
"No, no," said Grandpa.
"Just wet...
Then I heard a growl.

A huge polar bear came around
the corner.

I scrambled up a wall
of ice.

At the top were a lot of walruses.

I tried to lift one of the walruses.
It weighed about six thousand pounds

but I finally lifted it, and

threw it at the polar bear.

Then I ran away.

I still couldn't go to sleep, so I sat up
all night, watching the Northern Lights.

In the morning, the iceberg began to melt.

It got smaller and smaller.
Then I saw an island.

I swam ashore..."
"I bet you were sleepy,"
said Mary Ann.
"No, but I was a bit chilly,"
said Grandpa.

"Just as I started to get dry and warm,
I heard a noise…"

"What kind of noise?"
asked Mary Ann. "Like some
small bird or insect?"
"Or like something really big
and scary?" asked Louie.
"More like that," said Grandpa.

"The noise got louder. Smoke and fire came out of the jungle.
The ground was shaking.
Are you two getting sleepy?" asked Grandpa.
"No!" said Louie and Mary Ann. "What was it?"

"It was a huge dragon, breathing fire.

He chased me into the ocean.

All I could do was splash water at him.''

''I guess *that* didn't do any good,''
said Louie.
''Yes, it did,'' said Grandpa.

"It put his fire out, and

in all the smoke, I was able to escape.
But he ran after me.

I hid with some zebras, until the dragon went by. Then...

I swung through the jungle on vines, so as to avoid the crocodiles.

I could hear the dragon coming after me, so I climbed a very tall tree. I climbed and climbed and climbed…''

"Weren't you getting tired *yet?*" asked Mary Ann.
"Not in the least," said Grandpa.
"It was only a mile or so.

Finally I came to a small house
at the very top.

Inside the house was a dog…"
"Like ours?" said Louie.
"Exactly," said Grandpa.

"He was very friendly.

I sat down in a big, comfortable chair, and for the first time, I yawned."

"You did?" said Mary Ann.
"Like this?" said Louie, yawning.
"Exactly," said Grandpa.

"And then I shut my eyes, and that's when..."

the hurricane struck.''
''What hurricane?'' asked Mary Ann.
''The really big one,'' said Grandpa, ''that carried the house away.

We went racing across the ocean.

When we came to land, the house
headed for a mountain...

but the chair kept going.        We went down and down…

and through a window, into a house
just like this.

What do you think of *that?*"
asked Grandpa.

There was no answer.